This book belongs to:

_____

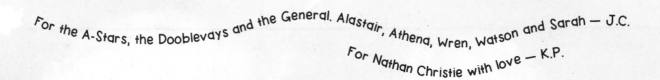

For the A-Stars, the Dooblevays and the General. Alastair, Athena, Wren, Watson and Sarah — J.C.

For Nathan Christie with love — K.P.

This paperback edition first published in 2020 by Andersen Press Ltd.

First published in Great Britain in 2018 by Andersen Press Ltd.,

20 Vauxhall Bridge Road, London SW1V 2SA.

Text copyright © Judy Corbalis, 2018.

Illustration copyright © Korky Paul, 2018.

The rights of Judy Corbalis and Korky Paul to be identified as the

author and illustrator of this work have been asserted by them in

accordance with the Copyright, Designs and Patents Act, 1988.

All rights reserved.

Printed and bound in Malaysia.

1 3 5 7 9 10 8 6 4 2

British Library Cataloguing in Publication Data available.

ISBN 978 1 78344 756 5

A big thank you to Longworth Undenominational Primary School, Oxfordshire for helping with the endpapers.

Front endpaper: Cooper Standley Young 10yrs and Imogen Gilbert 10yrs.

Back endpaper: Hannah King 9yrs and Joe Eighteen 6yrs.

Get that BALL

Judy Corbalis

Korky Paul

Andersen Press

One day, Tom and his granny were playing
penalty shoot-out when Granny's kick...

"Get that ball!" roared Granny
as it popped out by the pond
and flew over the fountain...

then bounced along the high street...

away out of town, up into the mountains...

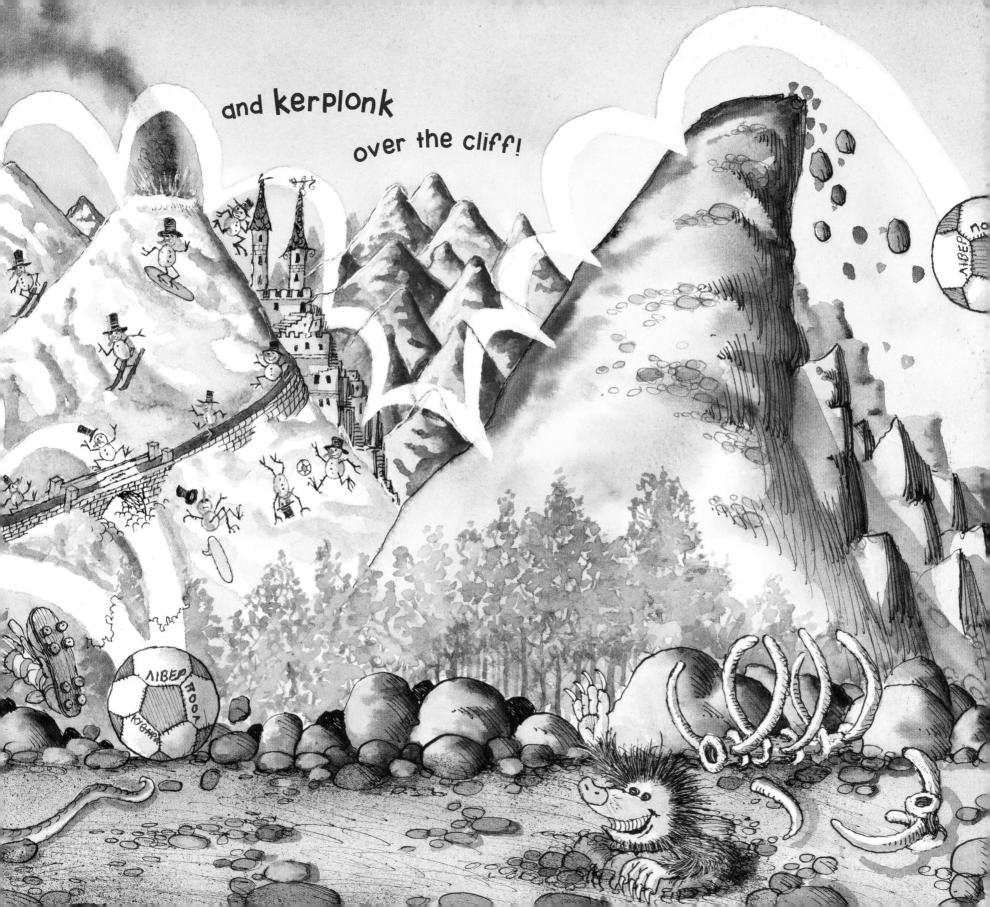

and sank into the sea.

"After it!" called Tom, diving into the deep, wild waves.

a gigantic bird swooped out of the sky and snatched the ball in its talons.

"No you don't!" bellowed Granny, grabbing Tom's boot.

Tom clung to the ball,
Granny clung to Tom,
and they flew...
and flew...

and flew...

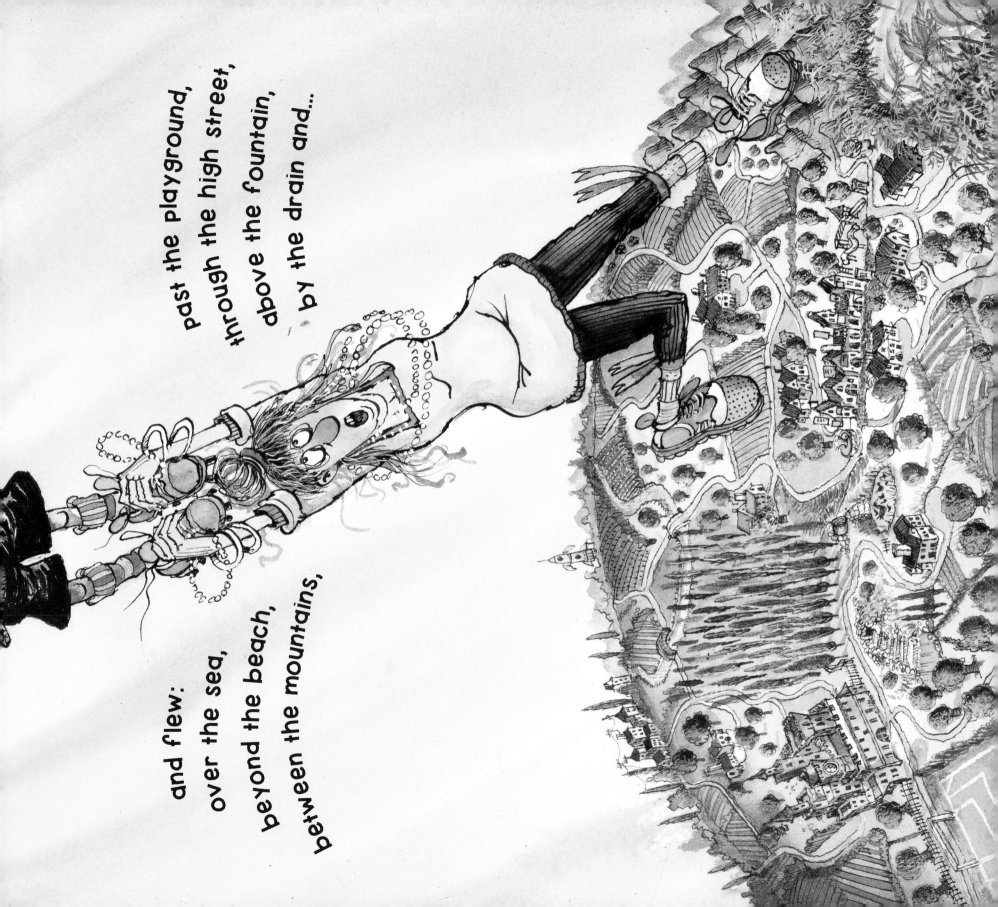

past the playground,
through the high street,
above the fountain,
by the drain and...

and flew:
over the sea,
beyond the beach,
between the mountains,

landed – **thwack** – on the football pitch.

"Beat it, bird!" shouted Granny.

"Right," said Tom, "my turn."
He lined up the ball, stepped back, raised his foot and...